Snowman Surprise

Adapted by Andrea Posner-Sanchez
from the script "Think Pink" by Ed Valentine

Based on the television series created by Chris Nee

Illustrated by Mike Wall

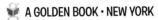 A GOLDEN BOOK · NEW YORK

Copyright © 2015 Disney Enterprises, Inc. All rights reserved. Published in the United States by Golden Books, an imprint of Random House Children's Books, a division of Penguin Random House LLC, 1745 Broadway, New York, NY 10019, and in Canada by Random House of Canada, a division of Penguin Random House Ltd., Toronto, in conjunction with Disney Enterprises, Inc. Golden Books, A Golden Book, A Little Golden Book, the G colophon, and the distinctive gold spine are registered trademarks of Penguin Random House LLC.
randomhousekids.com
ISBN 978-0-7364-3142-2 (trade) – ISBN 978-0-7364-3473-7 (ebook)
Printed in the United States of America
16 15 14 13 12 11 10 9 8

It's a beautiful winter afternoon, and Doc McStuffins
is playing in the snow with her toys.

"I just love when it snows!" Doc exclaims.

"Me too!" says Stuffy the stuffed dragon. "I love
everything about snow. . . ." Just then, a clump of snow falls
from a branch and lands on Stuffy's head.

"Except that."

Chilly, Doc's stuffed snowman, is excited to spend time with a real snowman. "Come on, you can tell me . . . you get cold sometimes, right? I know I d-d-do!" Chilly says with a shiver.

Doc giggles and reminds Chilly that unlike the real snowman, *he* has to bundle up in the cold.

Soon, Doc's dad calls for her to go inside. Doc scoops up Chilly, Lambie, Hallie, and Stuffy and walks to the house.

Once inside, Doc gets out of her **wet** clothes.
Her boots, mittens, and scarf are easy to take off,
but she needs a little help getting out of her jacket.

Doc runs upstairs to do her homework.
Her dad takes her wet clothes to the laundry room.
Neither of them notices that Chilly is missing.

After dinner, Doc's brother, Donny, shows off the diorama he made for school.

"It's a winter scene," explains Donny. "What do you think?"

Doc takes a look. "You know what it could use? A snowman! Do you want to borrow Chilly?"

"That would be cool!" says Donny.

Doc goes to her bedroom to get Chilly, but she doesn't see him. She holds her stethoscope until it glows, making her toys magically come to life.

"Have you seen Chilly?" Doc asks Stuffy, Hallie, and Lambie. "I know I brought him in the house."

Everyone looks around. No Chilly.

"Let's have a search party!" suggests Hallie.

Doc and the toys sneak downstairs. "You guys check the living room," Doc says. "I'll go to the laundry room."

Lambie peeks under a couch cushion.

Hallie looks inside a cabinet.

Stuffy peers behind a curtain. No Chilly.

"Chilly? Are you down here?"
Doc calls into the laundry room.
There is no answer. Then, just as
Doc leaves the room to continue
her search, her stethoscope glows.

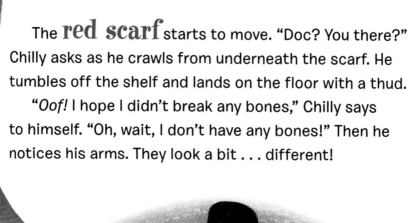

The **red scarf** starts to move. "Doc? You there?" Chilly asks as he crawls from underneath the scarf. He tumbles off the shelf and lands on the floor with a thud.

"*Oof!* I hope I didn't break any bones," Chilly says to himself. "Oh, wait, I don't have any bones!" Then he notices his arms. They look a bit . . . different!

Chilly rushes into Doc's bedroom. "Maybe it's not so bad," he says, trying to calm down. He nervously peeks at the mirror. "It's worse!" he shouts. "I'm pink all over!"

Chilly hears Doc and the others heading his way. "Oh, no! They'll laugh at me if they see me like this." He runs and hides.

"I'm worried about Chilly. Where could that snowman be?" Hallie asks as she and the others enter Doc's room.

"No need to worry," says Chilly. "Here I am!"

Doc and the toys turn to see Chilly's hat peeking from between some books. "I'm just tidying up back here," he explains.

"Well, I have exciting news," Doc says. "Donny needs a snowman for his project, and he wants you! You're perfect for it!"

Chilly is thrilled that Donny and Doc think he's the perfect snowman. But he's not perfect now—he's pink!

As Doc gets closer to the bookshelf, Chilly jumps into
the laundry basket. When he climbs out, he's wearing one of
Doc's socks. "*Brrrr, it's chilly in here,*" he says.

Doc kneels down. "Chilly, is something wrong?" she asks.
"Maybe I should give you a checkup."

Chilly leans closer to Doc and whispers, "There *is* something wrong, but I can't show you in front of everybody."

Doc asks Hallie, Stuffy, and Lambie to give them some privacy. "Okay, we're alone," says Doc. "And you know you can tell your doctor anything. So what's going on?"

Chilly takes off the sock. "This is the worst thing you've ever seen, right?"

Doc reassures Chilly as she examines him. "Everything's okay, except your color has changed," Doc says. "I think you have a case of pink-i-tosis. But don't worry. I'm going to fix you."

"I hope so," Chilly says with a sigh. "Donny needs a perfect snowman, and right now I'm not perfect at all."

"Just because you're different doesn't mean you're not perfect!" Doc declares. "Now, can you tell me what happened?"

Chilly starts to cry. "I have no idea! I woke up in the laundry room under your snow clothes and I was pink!"

"That's it!" Doc exclaims. "Dad must have washed you by accident, and the red color from my scarf rubbed off on you! We can get you cleaned up whenever you want!"

Chilly wants to tell everyone that he's okay, so he and Doc go over to the other toys. "No matter what color you are, we love you just the same!" says Hallie as his friends hug him.

Chilly is starting to like his new color. "Do you think Donny would mind a **pink snowman** in his project?" he asks Doc.

"Let's find out," she says.

Doc shows Chilly to her brother. "A pink snowman? Cool!" says Donny. "No one else is going to have a pink snowman in their project!"

The next day, Donny rushes home with great news.
"Guess what?" he shouts as he hands Chilly to Doc.
"My teacher said using a pink snowman was very creative.
And she gave me a gold star!"
"I'm so proud of you, Donny!" Doc tells her brother.
"And I'm proud of you, too," she whispers to Chilly.

A little later, Doc and her toys go outside to play. Chilly shows the real snowman a photo of himself with the gold star.

"You know, no one should be afraid to be different," Chilly says.

Doc walks over and smiles. "Ready for Dad to clean you now?" she asks.

Chilly nods. "Pink. Red. Green. It's not the color that makes you a snowman—it's the snow. Or, in my case, the stuffing!"